Thomas the Tank Engine & Friends®

A BRITT ALLCROFT COMPANY PRODUCTION

Based on The Railway Series by the Reverend W Awdry
© 2006 Gullane (Thomas) LLC
Thomas the Tank Engine & Friends and Thomas & Friends are trademarks
of Gullane Entertainment Inc.
Thomas the Tank Engine & Friends is Reg. U.S. Pat. TM Off.
A HIT Entertainment Company

www.randomhouse.com/kids   www.thomasandfriends.com

Library of Congress Cataloging-in-Publication Data
Blue train, Green train / illustrated by Tommy Stubbs. — 1st ed.
p.   cm. — (A bright and early book)
"Based on The Railway Series by The Reverend W. Awdry."
SUMMARY: Blue train Thomas works all day, and Green train Percy works all night.
ISBN 0-375-83463-X (trade) — ISBN 0-375-93463-4 (lib. bdg.)
[1. Railroads—Trains—Fiction. 2. Day—Fiction. 3. Night—Fiction. 4. Stories in
rhyme.] I. Stubbs, Tommy, ill. II. Awdry, W. Railway series. III. Series: Bright &
early book.
PZ8.3.B59853 2006   [E]—dc22   2005006754

Printed in the United States of America
First Edition 14 13 12 11 10
BRIGHT & EARLY BOOKS and colophon and RANDOM HOUSE and colophon
are registered trademarks of Random House, Inc.

Blue Train, Green Train

Illustrated by Tommy Stubbs

A Bright and Early Book
From BEGINNER BOOKS®

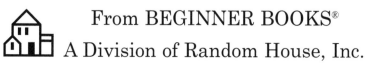

A Division of Random House, Inc.

Up comes the yellow sun!
Blue train Thomas starts his run.

Green train Percy sees the sun.
Now his busy run is done.

Well done, green train!
Have fun, blue train!

"Peep! Peep!" Clickety-clack!
Blue train Thomas on the track.

Load up the brown cows,

white eggs, green plows.

Load up the blue bikes, red wagons, orange trikes!

Load up the new toys,

gifts for little girls and boys!

The sun is yellow.
The sun is round.
The sun makes shadows
on the ground.

Here comes a gray cloud!
Blue train Thomas peeps so loud.

Down, down on the train,
gray clouds start to rain.
"Peep! Peep! Oh, no!"
Where can wet train Thomas go?

"Peep, peep!" The sun is back.
Blue train slows down on the track.
Unload the brown cows,
white eggs, green plows.

Unload the blue bikes,
red wagons, orange trikes!
Unload the new toys
for happy little girls and boys!

Down goes the yellow sun.
Blue train Thomas' day is done.
Home now to the Shed.
"Peep, peep!"
The Shed is where
Thomas can sleep.

Up peeps the white moon.
Green train starts soon.
"Peep! Peep!" Clickety-clack!
Green train Percy on the
track.

Load up all the mail
and unload along the rail.

Boxes of all shapes and sizes.
Blue presents, red prizes.

Cards and letters by the sack.
Lots of brown crates in a stack.

Green train Percy slows down.
He picks some up
and puts some down.
Boxes of all shapes and sizes.
Blue presents, red prizes.
Cards and letters by the sack.
Lots of brown crates in a stack.

The moon is round.
The moon is white.
The moon makes shadows
in the night.

The night is cool.
The fog is thick.
A yellow light
will do the trick.

Up peeps the yellow sun!
Green train Percy now is done.
Home now to the Shed.
"Peep, peep!"
The Shed is where
Percy can sleep.

Blue train sees the sun.
Time again to start his run!

Well done, green train.

Have fun, blue train.